Parents and Caregivers,

Stone Arch Readers are designed to provide enjoyable reading experiences, as well as opportunities to develop vocabulary, literacy skills, and comprehension. Here are a few ways to support your beginning reader:

- Talk with your child about the ideas addressed in the story.

- Discuss each illustration, mentioning the characters, where they are, and what they are doing.

- Read with expression, pointing to each word. You may want to read the whole story through and then revisit parts of the story to ensure that the meanings of words or phrases are understood.

- Talk about why the character did what he or she did and what your child would do in that situation.

- Help your child connect with characters and events in the story.

Remember, reading with your child should be fun, not forced. Each moment spent reading with your child is a priceless investment in his or her literacy life.

Gail Saunders-Smith, Ph.D

STONE ARCH **READERS**

are published by Stone Arch Books
151 Good Counsel Drive, P.O. Box 669
Mankato, Minnesota 56002
www.capstonepub.com

Library of Congress Cataloging-in-Publication Data
Crow, Melinda Melton.
    Mud mess / by Melinda Melton Crow ; illustrated by Ronnie Rooney.
    p. cm. — (Stone Arch readers)
    ISBN 978-1-4342-1622-9 (library binding)
    ISBN 978-1-4342-1753-0 (pbk.)
    [1. Dump trucks—Fiction. 2. Trucks—Fiction.] I. Rooney, Ronnie, ill. II. Title.
PZ7.C88536Mu 2010
[E]—dc22

                                                                  2008053405

Summary: Three truck buddies go out for a drive. See which truck gets stuck in the mud.

Creative Director: Heather Kindseth
Graphic Designer: Hilary Wacholz

Reading Consultants:
Gail Saunders-Smith, Ph.D
Melinda Melton Crow, M.Ed
Laurie K. Holland, Media Specialist

Printed in the United States of America in Stevens Point, Wisconsin.
122009
005645R

**The little bunny is a friend of the truck pals.
Every time you turn the page, look for it.
Can you find the little bunny?**

MUD MESS

written by
Melinda Melton Crow

illustrated by
Ronnie Rooney

STONE ARCH BOOKS
MINNEAPOLIS   SAN DIEGO

This is Green Truck.
This is Dump Truck.
This is Blue Truck.

Blue Truck goes up the hill.

Blue Truck goes down
the hill.

Green Truck goes up the hill.

Green Truck goes down the hill.

Dump Truck goes up the hill.
Here comes the rain.

15

Dump Truck goes in the mud.

Oh no!
Dump Truck is stuck in the mud.

Green Truck and Blue Truck
go up the hill again.

They see Dump Truck.
They want to help.

Green Truck and Blu
go up the hill again

They see Dump Truck
They want to help.

23

Green Truck and Blue Truck
pull Dump Truck out.

Dump Truck is out!

They go down the hill.
Now they are pals.

They are three truck pals!

STORY WORDS

truck	hill	mud
dump	rain	help

Total Word Count: 106

Follow your favorite truck pals as they learn about the open road.